ON LINE

For Lee

First Aladdin Paperbacks edition November 2000
Copyright © 1997 by Lisa Campbell Ernst
ALADDIN PAPERBACKS
An imprint of Simon & Schuster Children's Publishing Division
1230 Avenue of the Americas
New York, NY 10020

Also available in a Simon & Schuster Books for Young Readers hardcover edition.
Book design by Lisa Campbell Ernst. The text for this book was set in Goudy Old Style.
The illustrations were rendered in pastel, ink, and pencil.
Printed and bound in Hong Kong.
2 4 6 8 10 9 7 5 3 1
The Library of Congress has cataloged the hardcover edition as follows:
Ernst, Lisa Campbell. Bubba and Trixie / by Lisa Campbell Ernst. p.   cm. Summary:
An adventuresome ladybug befriends an apprehensive caterpillar and helps him learn to
enjoy life and be happy with what he is and what he becomes. [1. Ladybugs—Fiction.
2. Caterpillars—Fiction. 3. Friendship—Fiction. 4. Fear—Fiction.] I. Title.
PZ7.E7323Bu   1997[E]—dc20 96-35046 CIP   AC
ISBN 0-689-81357-0 (hc.)
ISBN 0-689-83851-4 (Aladdin pbk.)

BUBBA
and
TriXie

Lisa Campbell Ernst

Aladdin Paperbacks
New York   London   Toronto   Sydney   Singapore

Bubba was a 'fraidy cat.
A nervous Nelly. A tremble-toes.
And until the day Trixie came to
visit, he had never set even *one* of
his sixteen feet off the parsley
plant where he was born.

Bubba *wanted* to go out into the garden, but he was too scared. Bugs frightened him; flowers, the wind, and the rain all scared him—why, he was even scared silly of his own shadow.

"Have mercy!" Bubba shrieked when he saw Trixie for the first time. "Don't hurt me!"

Trixie laughed so hard
she tumbled from the leaf she
was standing on and landed
with a thud three leaves below.
"What have I done?"
Bubba hollered, and, forgetting
his fear, he hobbled down the
stem to see if the tiny
ladybug was still alive.

"Why didn't you fly? You're a *ladybug*!" Bubba wailed.
Trixie held up her right wing. "Wing's crimped,"
she said. "Never could fly."
Bubba gasped. "Never? Aren't
you scared you'll
be eaten?"
For an instant
Trixie looked
sadly at her wing.
"Hogwash!" she
snorted at last.
"What makes *you*
such a jittery scaredy-cat?"
"Take a look," whined Bubba.
"I can't fly or hop or even run—
I'm probably the biggest slowpoke in the
whole garden except for . . ." Bubba eyed Trixie.
"Me?" Trixie finished.
Bubba hung his head and began to cry. "But *I'm*
uglier than a clod of dirt and twice as clumsy!" he wept.
"I'm too scared even to leave this plant!"

"Now stop it," Trixie said. "You've *never* been out there?" She waved at the brilliant garden.

"Of course not!" Bubba sobbed. "I-I want to, but I can't—it's just too plain scary!"

Trixie studied the trembling caterpillar. "Well, it won't be scary with *me*," she said at last.

Bubba started to object, but Trixie stopped him. She pushed him to the edge of the leaf he was standing on, overlooking a huge bed of Corsican mint. "Hold my hand," ordered Trixie, "close your eyes, now JUMP."

And before he knew it, Bubba was hurtling through the air with a strange ladybug holding his hand.

When they landed on the mint below,
it was as soft as a new feather bed. Bubba swooned
from the excitement and the smell of mint that filled the air.
"Come," said Trixie, and she marched Bubba through the garden,
talking all the way. She named each of the flowers and plants and all the
insects and beasts that lived in their world. She taught Bubba how to

keep an eye out for birds, which plants
had stickers, and where the spiders hid.
Bubba marveled at the garden around him. With Trixie
at his side, he felt magically free, as if he could do anything at all.
"Now that I've taught you to be careful," said Trixie, "it's high
time I taught you how to have *fun*."

And from that moment on, life
was never the same for the two new friends.

Trixie taught Bubba how to play tag in the petunias
and hide-and-seek in the snapdragons.

On rainy days they slid down iris-leaf water slides and
sailed across puddles in magnolia leaves.

They played games with the roly-pollies, told jokes to
the grasshoppers, and sang songs with the bees and the beetles.

On windy days Trixie and Bubba could be seen riding tiger lilies like bucking broncos. On sunny days they made monster shadows in the grass.

No matter where they went in the garden, everyone knew who they were. "You two move slow as molasses," their friends agreed, "but you sure know how to kick up your heels."

Bubba never knew life could be so much fun. "Being a caterpillar is *grand*," he crowed.

The summer slowly unfolded
before them, one day after another.
    Each evening the two friends climbed to the highest
sunflower in the garden and watched as the sun set and the
fireflies appeared. They danced to the music of crickets in
the grass and made wishes on the stars above.
    Trixie's was the same each evening. "I wish I could
touch the stars," she whispered.

One August night Bubba, too, wished out loud. "I wish for everything to stay exactly as it is right now, *forever*."

A grasshopper chuckled nearby. "Of course that is impossible," he said. "It's nearly autumn, and life is about to change very much. Especially for *you*."

"What does he mean by that?" Bubba asked Trixie.

Trixie looked at her friend and smiled. "Surely you know, dear, that during the winter you will change into a butterfly."

Bubba stared back blankly.
"Absolutely not," he said.

"But that's what caterpillars *do*. They become butterflies," Trixie said gently. "That's just how it is."

Bubba's face turned pink. "Well not for *me*," he shouted. "I *like* being a caterpillar, I don't want to be a butterfly!" He stomped his feet.

A crowd was beginning to gather.

"But don't you see?" said the grasshopper. "As a butterfly, you'll be able to travel with great speed like me!"

"And fly like me!" buzzed a bee.

"And be beautiful like me," said a jewel beetle.

"And graceful like me," called a mayfly.

Bubba threw his arms around Trixie and cried. "But I don't *want* to change. I just want to stay me—and be your friend!"

"We'll *always* be friends," Trixie said.
"So what if you're a caterpillar *or* a butterfly?"
But Bubba refused to listen.
No matter what Trixie said, Bubba
insisted he would not change.
Weeks passed slowly.

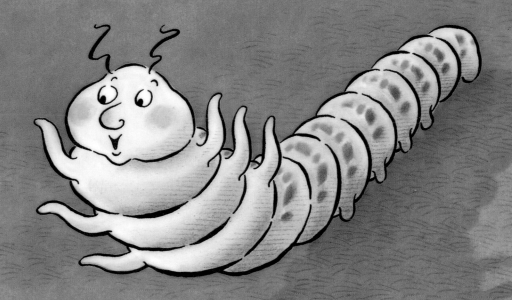

Then one chilly day Bubba gave
out a whoop. "I've got it! The perfect
plan so I will *never* become a butterfly!"
Trixie listened silently.

"I will build a house around myself," Bubba
declared. "So tight that I could not possibly change.
I will stay there all winter so that in spring I will be
the same—and we will be friends, just as always."

Trixie was quiet for a long time. "We will always
be friends," she whispered at last. "That I promise."

The next morning Bubba began
his project with great gusto. Climbing up
a parsley plant, he spun a button of silk to attach
himself. "It's odd," Bubba chuckled, "I've never built
a house before, but somehow I know just what to do."

"I think a caterpillar's house is called a cocoon,"
Trixie said quietly.

"Yes, well, whatever," mumbled Bubba,
continuing his work. "Now—where will *you* be?"

"Ladybugs sleep through the winter, too," Trixie
answered. "I'll be right below you, under the mint leaves."

"Perfect," Bubba said sleepily, suddenly exhausted.

Trixie settled between
the leaves. "See you in the
spring," she called. But before
Bubba could answer, the two
best friends had fallen asleep.

Winter came. The final
leaves fell from the trees, and soon
snow and ice covered the ground.
Trixie and Bubba were safe in
their winter beds, lost in dreams of
sunshine and snapdragons, sunsets
and the summer wishing stars.
Winter day followed winter day.

Then gradually the earth began to warm, the days to lengthen. Daffodils rose and flowered.

Trixie woke to spring's earthy smells and raced up the brown parsley plant to find Bubba's house.

"Bubba," she whispered, "are you in there?" Trixie pressed her ear against the cocoon but heard nothing. "Bubba!" she said louder. "Wake up, it's spring."

"Is that you, Trixie?" said a mumbly voice from inside.

"Of course it is. Please come out."

Very slowly, Bubba poked his sleepy head out of the cocoon, then struggled and squeezed the rest of the way out. "Hey, it worked," he croaked. "I'm still *me*!"

"Of course you are," Trixie answered, standing back for a better look. "You, with a bit more."

Bubba looked behind him and saw two very wet, crumpled butterfly wings. "But—why do I still feel like me?"

"Because you *are* still you," Trixie said. "Only the part on the outside changed. Don't you see? What's important is all on the inside, and that never changes. We will always be friends."

Bubba smiled slowly, looking again at his drying wings.

"Whoooeeee!" he shouted. "I'm downright gorgeous!"

He wiggled his wings in the light and danced a jig.

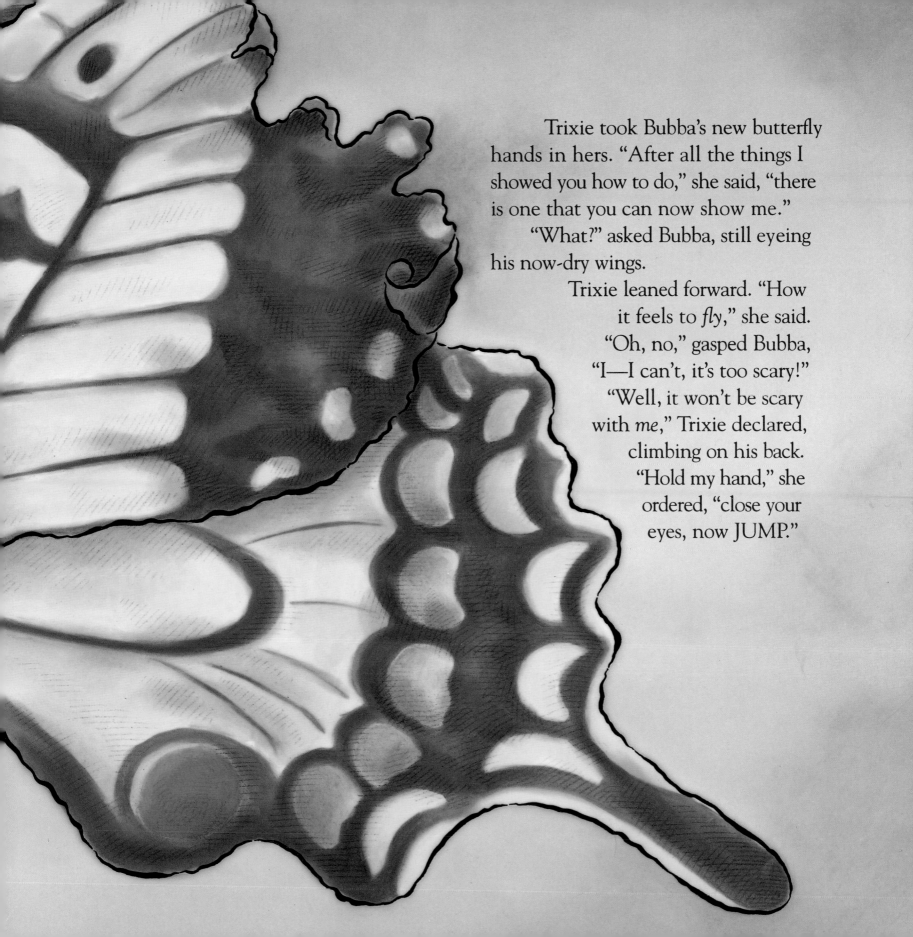

Trixie took Bubba's new butterfly hands in hers. "After all the things I showed you how to do," she said, "there is one that you can now show me."

"What?" asked Bubba, still eyeing his now-dry wings.

Trixie leaned forward. "How it feels to *fly*," she said.

"Oh, no," gasped Bubba, "I—I can't, it's too scary!"

"Well, it won't be scary with *me*," Trixie declared, climbing on his back. "Hold my hand," she ordered, "close your eyes, now JUMP."

And so Bubba stretched out his wings and jumped.
"Flutter!" called Trixie. For one perilous instant,
the two friends began to sink—Bubba flapped faster,
his tiny heart pounding. He was all caterpillar
bravery and butterfly razzle-dazzle.

Trixie held on for her life.

Then, oh, so slowly, the two
friends began to rise. A breeze caught
under Bubba's wings. "I'm flying!" he
shrieked with delight. "I'm still
me, and *I'm flying!*"

Down below, the garden
creatures looked up in amazement
toward the sound of laughing.
Higher and higher Bubba and
Trixie soared, until it seemed to
everyone that they could, indeed,
touch the newly emerging
wishing stars.

A Few Facts About Ladybugs and Caterpillars

Of course Bubba and Trixie are
imaginary, and so is the garden where they live.
Here, though, are a few facts:

Ladybugs and caterpillars both begin life in tiny eggs.
Once they have hatched, they spend most of their time eating
to grow larger. Swallowtail caterpillars eat plants like parsley and
dill. Ladybugs eat other insects such as aphids.

When they hatch, ladybugs are tiny larvae. They shed their skin
to become pupae and then become adult ladybugs about a
week later. As a caterpillar grows, it sheds its old, too-small skin
many times. When the time comes for it to become a butterfly, the
caterpillar sheds its skin once more, this time forming a protective
wall. Although a common name for its covering during this stage
is a cocoon, the actual name is a chrysalis. The transformation
for a swallowtail butterfly can take as little as three weeks,
but many swallowtails stay in the chrysalis stage all winter,
emerging the following spring. Ladybugs sleep throughout
the winter as well, finding a cozy tree hollow
or a pile of leaves for protection.

In the spring both ladybugs and butterflies lay
new eggs to begin the life cycle
all over again.